SHHHH!

Suzy Kline
pictures by Dora Leder

Albert Whitman & Company, Niles, Illinois

Text © 1984 by Suzy Kline
Illustrations © 1984 by Dora Leder
Published in 1984 by Albert Whitman & Company, Niles, Illinois
Published simultaneously in Canada
by General Publishing, Limited, Toronto
All rights reserved. Printed in U.S.A.
10 9 8 7 6 5 4 3 2

Library of Congress Cataloging in Publication Data

Kline, Suzy Weaver.
  SHHHH!

  Summary: Constantly hushed by all the older people
around her, a little girl finally goes outside and
lets loose with all the noises she knows.
  [1. Noise—Fiction] I. Leder, Dora, ill. II. Title.
PZ7.K6797Sh 1984   [E]   83-26032
ISBN 0-8075-7321-3

SH!" says my mother. "The baby is sleeping."

"SH!" says Grandma. "Your grandpa is napping."

"SH!" says my father. "I'm writing at my desk."

"SH!" says my brother. "I'm watching television."

"SH!" says my sister. "I'm studying for a test."

"SH!" says my auntie. "I'm counting all my stitches."

"SH!" says my uncle. "I'm playing a game of chess."

"SH!" says the teacher. "The children are working."

"SH!" says the librarian. "People are reading."

"SH!" says my grandpa. "A fish is nibbling on my line."

"SH!" says my sister. "Don't talk in church."

"SH!" says my mother. "I'm talking on the phone."

"SH!" says my father. "I'm talking to your mother."

So I tiptoe outside to my backyard.

No one is there but me.

And I . . .

YELL . . . and
SCREAM . . . and

WHISTLE . . . and JUMP!

YODEL . . . and
HOLLER . . . and

SHOUT . . . and THUMP!

BELLOW . . . and
ROAR . . . and

BARK . . . and WHOOP!

SCREECH . . . and
CHEER . . . and

SQUAWK . . . and SWOOP!

SHRIEK . . . and
SQUEAK

. . . and
CRY OUT LOUD—

YIPPEE YAY HEY HEY!
YIPPEE YAY HEE HEE!

It's a RAH RAH DAY
for ME!
ME!
ME!

After I do that, I don't mind if I have to be quiet again.